I0712686

The Glass Ceiling:

Systematic Barriers to the Promotion of Women in the U.S. Navy

By

Millicent Marie Lowe

DECLARATION

I, Millicent Marie Lowe, declare that the contents of this thesis represent my own unaided work and that the thesis has not previously been submitted for academic examination towards any qualification. Furthermore, it represents my own opinions and not necessarily those of the University.

Signed   Abstract

The Promotion of Women in The Navy   Date

The study examines the trends associated with the promotion of women in the U.S. Navy's combat and administrative roles and demonstrates that women service members face systematic barriers to promotion. In spite of the difficulty of recruiting enough personnel for the All-

Volunteer Force (AVF) and a general ethic of equality, U.S. women are still barred from ground combat and are limited in their opportunities to ascend to higher ranks. Indeed, while women constitute 15 percent of Navy personnel, they only make up 7 percent of high-ranking officers.

The study will apply statistical analysis using multivariate regression models and qualitative analysis of Navy practices. The analysis of all three multivariate regression models indicates that the commissioning source is a significant determinant of retention and promotion for the SW community. While OCS graduates demonstrate the highest probability of remaining in the SW community, USNA graduates exhibit the lowest probability. Although USNA graduates were initially expected to have higher promotion rates, the results suggest that they are less likely to be promoted to the grade of O-4 than officers commissioned through NROTC-contract graduates.

However, they have a higher probability of promotion than officers from OCS, NROTC Regular, and other sources.

ABOUT THE AUTHOR

Millicent M. Lowe is a proud U.S. Navy and Army National Guard veteran with a lifelong dedication to service and leadership. With over three decades of experience in operations management and team development, she has built a career rooted in discipline, integrity, and results.

She has fought three wars in her active years in the military, namely, Desert Storm/Desert Shield, the 9/11 War on Terrorism, and was one of the key figures of Operation Enduring Freedom. Not only this, but Millicent Lowe was also an honored member of Cambridge's Who's Who.

Millicent earned her Bachelor's degree in Political Science from Pace University and later completed her MBA in Managerial Leadership at Nyack College. Her academic work includes research on the barriers women face in military advancement, reflecting her passion for equity and progress.

Throughout her professional journey—including her long tenure at the U.S. Postal Service — she has been recognized for her commitment to excellence, mentoring, and continuous improvement. Millicent brings the same determination and purpose to every endeavor she pursues.

Millicent has also gained experience by traveling all over the world during her military tenure, including places like Hawaii, England, France, Italy, Cuba, Guam, South Africa, Saudi Arab, and many more, all of which have helped her become the person that she is today.

She was stationed aboard the USS Puget Sound AD – 38, (Destroyer Tender) 1988 through 1992, Norfolk, Virginia. She also served as a Reservist at Ft. Schuyler, Bronx, New York and Floyd Bennett Field, Brooklyn, New York, Naval Reserve Readiness Center.

Table of Contents

CHAPTER I: INTRODUCTION

Women have made great strides in gaining inclusion and recognition in the U.S. Navy, one of the nation's oldest and most distinguished military branches. Despite the laudable contributions of women officers in the Navy, their involvement continues to be marred by marginalization and exclusion from leadership positions. It is a great advancement that women have been given the opportunity to serve alongside their male counterparts in defending the sovereignty and security of the nation. However, gender inequality also has contributed to a "glass ceiling," limiting women from being promoted to superior positions. Looking at statistics for the Marines and the Air Force, especially between the ranks of captain (0-3) and lieutenant colonel (0-5), Evertson and Nesbitt (2004) found that the reduced number of women leaders perpetuate a "glass ceiling" which, in turn, generates a "domino effect on the ambitions junior women develop in their careers." In fact, women tend to be regarded as having a need to be protected; consequently, their membership is restricted to certain non-combative positions.

Evidence from a study examining the treatment of the sexes across various Navy pay grades (Golan et al., 2010) appears to strengthen the "glass ceiling" perception. In times of combat, the gaps at specific pay grades (E-4 and E-5) increased between men and women not only because of changes in sex coefficients but also "because the average characteristics of women became less attractive relative to the Navy than those of men." Nevertheless, all individuals who wear a military uniform are conscious of the fact that their service may require the taking of a life or even the sacrifice of their own. Yet, these studies suggest that while some individual attributes or factors may apply on a case-by-case basis, no other characteristic than sex or race appears to play the consistently observed dominating role in determining promotions.

This research was conducted to determine the dynamics involved in the promotion of women and their merited contribution within the Navy. The recognition and promotion of women can be evaluated by their leadership qualities and ranking positions. Research shows that even highly trained, well-qualified women are not always given the same opportunity to advance in rank as their male counterparts, thereby accounting for a systematic gender disparity that must be addressed.

The United States has five military branches: the Army, the Air Force, the Marine Corps, the Navy, and the Coast Guard, the last of which is distinguished for its relative lack of barriers toward women's full involvement. However, this literature review will only consider the first four branches named above.

Some women were involved as nurses in the Civil War, and more than a thousand women nurses served during the Spanish-American War. In World War I, nurses served abroad, some near the front line, and the U.S. Navy made some women regular, although temporary members.

(Many of these were badly needed telephone operators.) World War II brought large numbers of women into the military, although they numbered less than two percent of the total. The vanguard was the nurses. A plan to draft nurses was aborted after being made public, but its revelation prompted a sufficient number of nurses to sign up for service voluntarily.

After World War II, for the first time, women became regular members of the peacetime force. However, there were limitations. The head of the nurse corps and the director of the women's corps, the WACs (Women's Army Corps members), WAVES (Women Accepted for Voluntary Emergency Service [Navy]), and WAFS (Women in the Air Force), could only temporarily hold the rank of colonel (Army, Air Force, Marine Corps) or captain (Navy).

Otherwise, women were limited to the position rank of lieutenant colonel or commander. The total number of women was not to exceed two percent of the force, and not more than ten percent of women could serve as officers. A 1951 executive order authorized the discharge of any woman. Who became pregnant or who had any child in her home for more than 30 days a year.

Furthermore, women could not exercise command authority over men. For instance, aboard a battleship, the commanding officer would not be permitted to be female.

Many changes occurred in the early 1970s. The draft ended in 1973. At the same time, in the civilian sphere, the ratification of a proposed equal rights amendment to the U.S. Constitution (which ultimately failed) appeared imminent. The military services suddenly discovered they needed women to fill their ranks. Civilian pressure to make women full participants in the military increased. The Navy and Army responded by allowing women to fly non-combat planes, and the Air Force, after delaying for several years, eventually followed suit. Women were allowed to attend the war colleges, which prepared officers for senior ranks and the U.S military.

Congress ordered women's admission to the military academies. Further, the U.S. Supreme Court ruled that discharge for pregnancy was unconstitutional, which increased the likelihood that a woman officer could have a sufficiently lengthy career needed to reach the upper ranks. By 1980, all of the separate women's corps had been abolished, and women had to compete with their male peers for promotion.

In the U.S. today, some men and women are uncomfortable with women's involvement in military roles. Despite the difficulty of recruiting enough members for an all-volunteer force (AVF), women remain barred from ground combat. However, since 1993, women have been allowed to serve in combat aviation and, since 1994, on most combat ships (They are still excluded from submarines for privacy reasons).

As of 2010, women constituted about 15 percent of U.S. military personnel, an all-time high. Women servicemembers are distributed across a range of specialties. Women can fill 99 percent of U.S. Air Force positions and more than 90 percent of U.S. Navy positions.

However, even though they can fulfill 93 percent of U.S. Army specialties because they cannot serve in combat specialties, their actual eligibility only applies to 70 percent of Army slots (Manning, 2008, p. 15). The continued constraints on women's full participation (especially in combat positions) contribute to the perception of women as unfit for leadership roles. Additionally, the fact that high-ranking women are generally leading divisions composed mostly of men, who may doubt the competency of their female superiors, represents a further challenge to their leadership.

The following is a list of the most commonly used acronyms and their full designations:

AVF: All-Volunteer Force

Enlisted Rates: E-1 to E-3 (Apprentice); E-4 to E-6 (Petty Officers and Non- commissioned Officers); E-7 to E-9 (Chief Petty Officer, Senior Chief Petty Officer, and Master Chief Petty Officer).

NCO: Non-commissioned Officer (e.g., W-1 Officer Rank: Warrant Officer).

NROTC: Naval Reserve Officer Training Corps.

OCS: Officer Candidate School.

Officer Ranks: W-2 to W-5 (Chief Warrant Officers); O-1 to 0-4 (Junior Officers: Ensign, Lieutenant [junior grade], Lieutenant, and Lieutenant Commander); O-5 and O-6 (Senior Officers: Commander and Captain).

SWO: Surface Warfare Officer.

CHAPTER II: LITERATURE REVIEW II

Statistics

Until 1988, women represented less than four percent of senior enlisted personnel. Since then, the percentage of women has regularly increased in each service. As FY 2008 began, for example, women made up 11 percent of senior Army personnel in pay grades 7, 8, and 9; seven percent of senior Navy personnel; five percent of Marine Corps members, and 13 percent of senior enlisted personnel in the Air Force (Manning, 2008, p. 17). The Army's 11 percent of women non-commissioned officers (NCOs) versus the 13 percent figure for overall female enlistment suggests an underrepresentation of women in the higher ranks.

As women comprise almost 15 percent of enlisted Navy personnel, the Navy's relatively low seven percent figure represents a significant decrease with elevated rank. This may be partly attributed to sea duty rotation requirements that may be experienced as being more onerous by women than by men. The five percent of senior women NCOs in the Marine Corps is only minimally disproportionate to the total six percent of enlisted women. However, in the Air Force, there is a notable disparity in that 20 percent of enlisted members are women, while only 13 percent of senior NCOs are women. This demonstrates the phenomenon known commonly as "the higher the fewer."

The 314 women E-9s in the Army, as of late 2007, represented almost nine percent of those holding that rank. Thus, the percentage of women fell even from E-7 to E-9.

Navy women made up six percent of the E-9s, Marine Corps women were four percent, and Air.

Force women, ten percent (Office of the Secretary of Defense, N.D.). For the sake of comparison, in the early 1980s, women represented less than two percent of O-6s, colonels, and Navy captains. (Manning, 2008, p. 17). Since then, the change has been dramatic but slow. It takes more than 20 years to become eligible for promotion to O-6, and many women were de facto barred from that rank by virtue of exclusion from the kind of responsible assignments that would lead to an O-6 promotion. By 2007 however, Army women constituted about 12 percent of the O-6s.

The Navy percentage was only slightly lower, while that of the Air Force was slightly higher. The Marine Corps' three percent reflects the fact that the Marines are essentially an all-combat force.

Commissioning Programs

There are various ways for women to become commissioned officers in the Navy. (Table 1). A college degree is the foremost requirement, and there exists a particular demand for those with engineering or scientific degrees. Individual background and personal characteristics also play a role. An officer's commission is an appointment by the U.S. president. There are two types of commission: regular and reserve. A regular commissioned officer commits to serve in the military full-time; a reserve commission may be full-time or part-time. Every officer graduating from one of the commissioning sources receives a reserve commission.

In order to become an officer, an individual may join one of the four commissioning sources:

1. The United States Naval Academy (USNA)

2. The Navy Reserve Officer Training Corps (NROTC)

3. Officer Candidate School (OCS)

4. Enlisted-to-officer commissioning programs

Table 1. Typical Methods of Becoming an Officer in the Military
(Adapted from Thirtle, 2001)

Entry Point	Pathways
High School	Enlisted College Military Preparatory School
Service Academy	Officer Candidate/Training School Reserve Officer Training Corps Direct Appointment

Career Development

According to Carman (2008), although the typical SWO career path was standardized and deviations from the norm were discouraged, the current career path has added flexibility and alternative opportunities, due to changing requirements in the SWO community. When officers earn a commission in the Navy and begin their career path as a career-designated SWO, they report immediately to a surface ship. They do not attend any formal school; instead, they are expected to learn their job through on-the-job training (OJT).

A newly commissioned officer generally spends a total of 45 months during his first and second division officer (DIVO) tours. Upon completing the first and second DIVO tours, the officer reaches an exit port, where he has to decide to stay or leave active military service at the 48-month mark (60 months for USNA graduates). If he decides to stay, he has two options: not taking the SWO retention bonus, while signing on for a two- to three-year shore-duty

The promotion of women in the navy assignment, or taking the SWO bonus and obligating himself for the next six years as a Navy officer, SWO (Browning & Burr, 2009).

Recruiting and Retention

As an organization, the U.S. Navy has to compete for manpower with civilian organizations and companies and other military branches. To attract and retain talent, the Navy must offer competitive wages as well as tangible and intangible benefits. Wages consist of basic pay, allowances, special and incentive pay, annual pay adjustments, and tax advantages (Carman, 2008). Tangible benefits include medical and dental care and reduced-cost life insurance policies. Intangible benefits include military-specific and general training, education, and the opportunity to serve one's country. The entry port for the Navy is the accession source. As aforementioned, several avenues exist for attaining commission. Because lateral entry is extremely limited due to the specificity of most military skills, recruiting high-quality officers at the entry level is highly crucial (Asch & Warner, 2001). However, the task of recruiting quality officers can be tough, as the Navy must compete with civilian and other governmental organizations for the same talent pool.

Military and civilian organizations have always been challenged in retaining their personnel. An employee's departure from an organization may be costly; consequently, organizations focus considerable attention on avoiding unwanted disruption caused by attrition (Clemens, 2002). Attrition is more problematic for the military than for other organizations. Due to the military's hierarchical personnel system, personnel separations have a much greater impact on organizational performance and stability than what would be observed in a civilian organization. In the Navy, middle- and senior-grade officers cannot be replaced by civilians.

Instead, they must be filled through promotions of junior officers. An investment of both time and financial resources is required before and after commissioning to produce a qualified and experienced officer. Moreover, attrition reduces officer quality, productivity, and recruitment.

(Clemens, 2002). Therefore, many studies have analyzed which commissioning source is most effective in retaining officers' promotions. Because there is no lateral entry opportunity, the Navy heavily depends on its promotion system to find qualified officers for its senior ranks. While SWOS are promoted through lieutenant (0-3) depending on their qualifications, minimum time in rank, and minimum time in service. They are selected by statutory boards for subsequent ranks based on their performance and background (Asch & Warner, 2001). According to Carman (2008), officers' worth increases as they are promoted to higher levels due to increased human capital and the importance of high-level assignments. This creates an inverse relationship between available personnel and the value of individual members (Table 2).

Table 2. Inverse Relationship Between Officer Inventory and Officer Value by Rank

(Adapted from Carman, 2008)

Officer Rank	Inventory Level	Value to Navy
O-1	High	Low
O-2	High	Low
O-3	Medium	Moderate
O-4	Medium	Moderate–High
O-5	Low	High
O-6	Very Low	Very High
O-7 to O-10	Extremely Low	Exceptional/Strategic

Table 2. This table illustrates the inverse relationship between officer inventory and the value of officers to the Navy, where higher-ranking officers are fewer in number but carry greater institutional value. *(Carman, 2008)*

The Navy's statutory officer promotion boards convene annually and select qualified officers for promotion to O-4 and higher levels based on the quality of their service records. The precept is a document approved by the convening authority and directed to the president of the board (Rogers & Grose, 2003), which provides general and specific guidance to the statutory board regarding the criteria upon which their selections should be based. The precept provides several important factors for the board to take into consideration, such as board membership, promotion percentages, and any specific guidance for the Navy's special needs at that time. While gender is not explicitly a factor, the precept may introduce criteria tangentially related to gender. Such as combat experience, for which women are officially denied.

Asch and Warner (2001) suggest that individuals are evaluated on both ability and work effort during the promotion process. The statutory boards take into account both these characteristics, which are written in service records, while selecting officers for promotion.

However, sometimes unobserved factors may also affect promotion decisions. Promotion boards consider officers who are fully qualified and then select those who are "best qualified." Fully-qualified officers are able to perform the duties of the next-higher pay grade. While best-qualified status is assigned to officers following evaluation in the following four areas (Carman,2008): proven and sustained performance, education, personal and professional development

- Ability to meet statutory promotion objectives, achievement of competency, and skill requirements

According to Carman (2008), there is a limited number of openings for senior-ranking officers, due to the hierarchical structure of the Navy. Beginning with the rank of lieutenant commander (0-4), the Navy limits the number of officers to be promoted to the next rank. Based on this restriction, the promotion system acts as a contest in which officers compete with their peers for a limited number of promotion slots (Carman, 2008).

Promotion Zones and Promotion Timing

Carman (2008) explains that eligibility for promotion is determined by the U.S. Secretary of the Navy's annual promotion plan. This sets up promotion zones for surface warfare officers. Promotion zones are the number of officers needed to fill projected personnel requirements and are established for each grade and competitive category. They categorize which officers are eligible for evaluation for promotion to a specific grade, based on lineal seniority. Zone size is a function of promotion opportunity. Promotion-zone opportunity is calculated as the number to be recommended for promotion divided by the number of officers in a promotion zone. Officers are categorized as "in zone," "below zone," and "above zone," as follows (Carman, 2008).

Above-zone: Officers in this zone have been previously reviewed in the in-zone population but were not selected for promotion by the board.

In-zone: Officers in this zone include the primary population eligible for consideration by the selection board.

Below-zone: Below-zone officers are junior to other officers in the promotion zone. If not selected, these officers do not incur a failure of selection. This group is a rough estimate of the following year's in-zone population.

According to Carman (2008), Title 10 of the USC limits the number of below-zone officers that can be selected to ten percent of the "authorized to select" pool number. Officers who are "below zone" and "above zone" may be considered for promotion, as approved by the promotion of women in the Navy.

U.S. Secretary of the Navy (Carman, 2008). The promotion timing and promotion opportunities or promotion to lieutenant, junior grade (0-2) through captain (0-6) are exhibited in the figure below.

Because promotion to a higher rank assumes increased responsibility and qualification for higher-level job assignments.

The SWO promotion system basically aims to promote the most qualified officers to ensure a good person-job fit. In this system, promotion plays two important roles. On the one hand, it tries to ensure a good person-job fit based on ability, and on the other hand, it encourages officers to improve their performance in pursuit of promotion (Fairburn & Malcomson, 2001). Theoretically, officers who do not have the required qualifications for the next rank cannot be selected for promotion.

However, because promotion opportunities at mid-grade promotion boards are significantly higher, with a promotion opportunity of up to 90 percent, and the eligible pool for promotion is larger than other boards, there exists a possibility that some officers who are not ready to accept the responsibility of higher rank may be selected nevertheless (Yardley et al., 2005). According to Carman (2008), the surface warfare community is more exposed to this scenario because the SWO inventory gap is larger than that of other communities at the mid-grade and senior ranks. For example, assume that an annual O-4 board is considered a hundred.

SWOS for promotion, only 75 of whom possess the qualifications required for the position of lieutenant commander (0-4). Because of the inventory gap in the SWO community at the O-4 level, the board precept would offer to select 90 percent of eligible officers.

CHAPTER III: METHODOLOGY

Research Method

The research is based on secondary data collection. The data are extracted from various journals, articles, and books. Secondary research describes information gathered through literature, publications, broadcast media, and other non-human sources, and does not involve human subjects. The research approach used is qualitative. Qualitative research is much more subjective than quantitative research and applies sharply different methods of collecting information, which could originate from both primary and secondary sources. As already mentioned, this study utilizes the secondary research method. The nature of this type of research is exploratory and open-ended, often less costly than conducting surveys, and is extremely effective in acquiring information. It is often the method of choice in instances where quantitative measurement is not required.

The study uses multivariate regression models for the analysis of retention and promotion. Regression analysis is applied to estimate the impact of the explanatory variables on the dependent variable as they change (holding all other variables constant). Two regression models are specified to find whether there is any relationship between the commissioning source and job performance, using retention and promotion as performance measures. In order to isolate the effect of the commissioning source on retention or promotion, the study controls for other independent variables that represent personal demographics and professional background, in addition to the commissioning source variables. The first retention model analyzes the effect of the commissioning source on retention decisions at the end of the minimum service requirement.

The data include variables for those who left after promotion to O-3. It also includes data on the promotion of women in the Navy officers who appeared before the O-4 Promotion Board. "Leavers" were defined as those who were promoted to 0-3 but did not appear at the O-4 promotion board. This is also used to code the "Stay" variable, which applies to retention models. The "Promote" variable takes the value of 1 for those who were promoted to O-4. Data includes officers who started the commissioning service between the years 1994 to 2004. Officers who graduated after 2004 were still expected to reach the O-4 promotion point at the time the data were extracted. STATA software was used to estimate the models.

Data Description

The data for this analysis were obtained from the Officer Master File (OMF) via the Navy Econometric Modeling (NEM) online data system. It contains 10,295 observations. All observations include surface warfare officers between fiscal years 1994 through 2009.

Observations after fiscal year 2004 were dropped from the data because these officers had yet to reach the O-4 career point at the time the data was collected. Variables that are used in the model are explained in detail in the following section.

Variables
Performance Measures

Performance measures are dichotomous dependent variables that indicate whether an individual achieved a particular goal or not. For the retention model, this dependent variable is "Stay." It takes a value of 1 if the individual remains up to the O-4 promotion board and 0 if he/she departed the Navy before that point. For the promotion model, the dependent variable is "Promote." It takes a value of 1 if the individual ascends to O-4 and 0 otherwise. Table 1 below

The promotion of women in the Navy depicts retention and promotion rates by commissioning sources. Note that these numbers are derived only from officers who were promoted to O-3. Officers who left before the O-3 promotion point were omitted from the remainder of the analysis.

The first column in the "Retention" panel shows the number of officers promoted to 0-3.

The second column represents the proportion of officers who stayed in service until the O-4 promotion board. Similarly, in the "Promotion" panel, the first column indicates the number of officers who stayed until the O-4 promotion board. The second column indicates the proportion of officers who received promotion to O-4. The retention numbers are highest for NROTC- regular and USNA (N in promotion), followed by OCS. However, promotion rates (the mean for promotion) are highest for OCS and NROTC contracts, followed by other sources. The total number shows that out of 7,262 officers promoted to O-3, 3,236 stayed in service until the O-4 promotion board. In addition, the promotion rate to O-4 for this group is 58.59 percent.

Commissioning Sources

Commissioning sources are broken down into the following categories: "USNA," "NROTC-regular," "NROTC-contract," "OCS," and "other sources" (Table 1). USNA, NROTC-regular, and NROTC-contract represent the graduates from their respective sources. OCSS consists of graduates from the Officer Candidate School and the Naval Officer Candidate program. Other sources are few in number and are grouped in the "other sources" variable. These sources include but are not limited to the USN Integration Program, commissioning directly from the Air Force Academy, and USA commissioned status.

Table 3. Retention and Promotion Rates by Commissioning Source

Commissioning Source	Retention N	Mean	SD	Promotion N	Mean	SD
USNA	2,630	0.5	—	966	0.535	0.499
NROTC Regular	—	0.523	0.605	1,007	0.49	0.5
NROTC Contract	256	0.641	0.481	118	0.754	0.432
OCS	1,230	0.745	0.436	665	0.786	0.410
Other Sources	849	0.677	0.468	—	0.571	0.495
Total	7,262	0.6087	0.488	3,236	0.5859	0.4926

Figure 3 below shows the distribution of graduates from each commissioning source over fiscal years. It is expected that USNA and NROTC-regular graduates are more likely to remain in service until the O-4 promotion board, but this affiliation has less effect on promotion to O-4.

There is a relative increase in the number of OCS graduates between the years 2001 and 2004.

This may be an effect of policy change by the Navy in an effort to respond quickly to the needs of the "Global War on Terrorism." In addition, graduates from "other sources" constituted large numbers during 1997 and 1999 for this ten-year term.

Figure 3 — Commissioning Source Distribution Over Fiscal Years

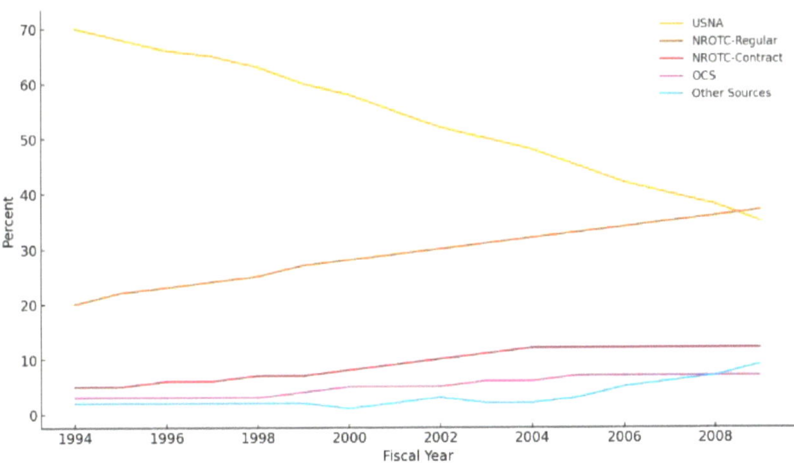

Marital Status

Women are divided into four groups according to their marital status: single without children, single with children, married without children, and married with children (Figure 4). This study theorizes that married officers will perform better based on prior studies that have demonstrated a "marriage premium" (Bowman & Mehay, 1999).

Figure 4 — Marital Status Distribution Over Fiscal Years

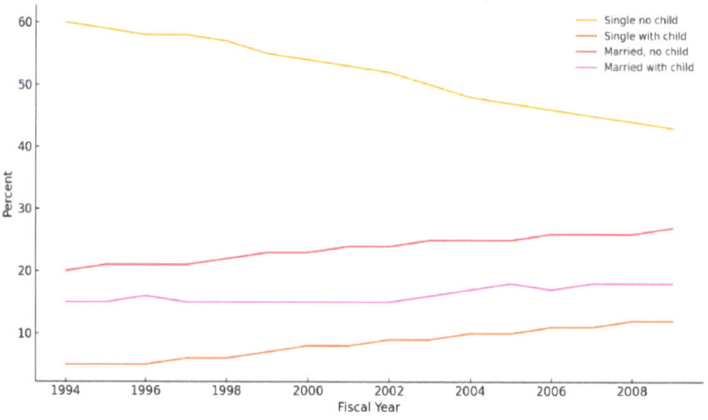

Race

Four different categories for race are included in the model: white, black, Asian, and other races (Figure 5). Racial distribution over time is shown in the figure below and appears relatively stable. Based on prior studies, it is expected that non-white officers will have a lower probability than whites of retention to O-4, but promotion rates will be higher if they remain in service.

Figure 5 — Race Distribution Over Fiscal Years

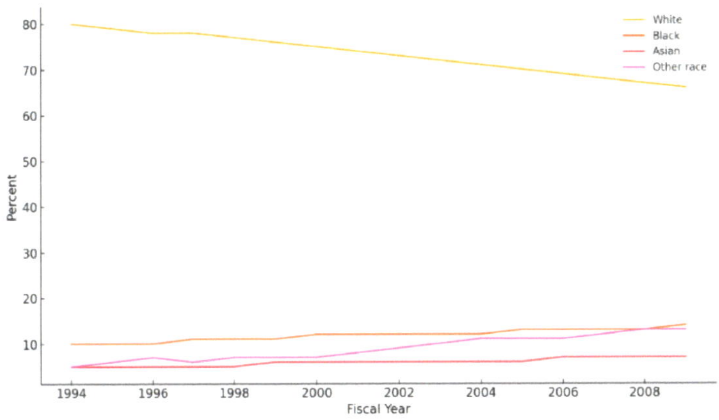

Educational Level

Educational level serves as a good proxy for ability and other unobservable characteristics. The educational level of officers varies from less than two years of college to a completed master's degree. Individuals with missing educational level information are also included in the model to mitigate any sample selection bias, as it is suspected that they may be systematically different from other officers. Figure 6 shows educational level distribution over time. There is an increase in the number of officers who either do not report their educational level or whose data are missing in the repository.

Figure 6 — Education Level Distribution Over Fiscal Years

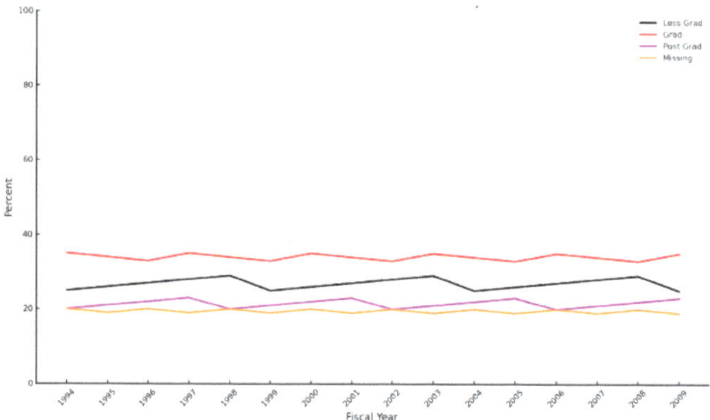

University Major

This variable represents officers' majors at a university or college, classified into five groups: life/health/medical sciences, physical sciences, engineering sciences, humanitarian sciences, and management/economics. Figure 7 shows the distribution of majors over commissioning sources. Among reported cases, there were 3,998 officers with technical majors and 4,729 non-technical majors. Between the years 1994 to 2009, human science and engineering majors were the most popular, with 2,915 and 2,655 officers, respectively. Physical science and management/economics follow, with 1,304 and 1,050 officers, respectively. It is assumed that while university majors have an effect on retention, they are exogenous to promotion. Majors are used in retention models, but not in the promotion models estimated below.

Figure 7 — University Majors' Distribution Over Commissioning Sources

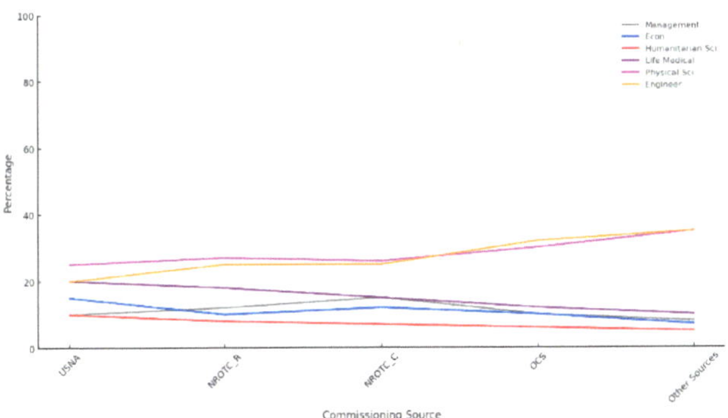

In other words, if the promotion probabilities of those who depart (i.e., had they stayed) are more than or less than those of officers who remain, then the promotion model would suffer from self-selection bias. In order to overcome such a problem, Heckman's self-selection model is utilized. This model involves a two-step procedure in which the first step includes predicting the determinants of survival. The second step incorporates this prediction and adjusts the estimates to take into account the nonrandom selection of the regression sample. In the study, the probit and Heckman's correction models are utilized to predict the effects of explanatory variables on retention and promotion.

Analysis-Based Models

The probit model is utilized to predict the retention model because the expected outcome is dichotomous. The retention model uses the "Stay" variable as a dependent variable. Independent variables include those representing commissioning sources, gender, race, marital status, educational background, and prior enlisted service. Also, year dummies are included in the model to control for other unobservable characteristics of cohorts and socio-economic conditions.

$\beta 9$other_race +

In (stay) = 30 + $\beta 1$nrote_r+ B2nrotc_c + B30cs + $\beta 4$other_src +

$\beta 5$prior_enlisted + $\beta 6$female + black + $\beta 8$asian+

$\beta 10$single_with_child+B11married_no_child

+

$\beta 12$married_with_chil d

+

$\beta 13$post grad + $\beta 14$life_medic_sci + $\beta 15$phy_sci + $\beta 16$hum_sci

+$\beta 17$mgt_econ + $\beta 17$fiscal years + ε

The promotion model initially utilizes probit regression to predict the probability of promotion to O-4. The dependent variable is "Promote," which is a binary variable. Independent

The promotion of women in the Navy variables are the same as for the retention models, with the exception of variables that represent the university majors of officers. We assume that these variables are exogenous to the promotion model but should be included in the retention model. This hypothesis is also the basis for the

Heckman sample-selection models.

In (promote)

Boß1nrotc_r+ ß2nrote_c + B30cs + ß4other_src + B5prior enlisted + ß6female + black +

ß8asian

B10single_with_child + + B9other_race +

ß11married_no_child + ß12married_with_child +

ß13post grad + ß17fiscal years + &

The Heckman model is built on the hypothesis that officers who left before the O-4 promotion board may differ in their promotion probabilities from those who stayed. The model first estimates the likelihood of remaining in service, then predicts the probability of promotion as if the entire sample before the promotion board had been observed. The "Promote" and "Stay" variables are two dichotomous variables for promotion and retention. Independent variables are the same as simple probit models; the only difference is that the retention model includes university majors, which are hypothesized to be endogenous for retention, but exogenous for the promotion model.

In (promote)

=

BO + Binrotc_r + B2Nrote_c + B30cs + ß4other_src +

B5prior_enlisted + ß6female + black + ß8asian

+

B9other_race +

B10single_with_child + B11married_no_child + B12married_with_child

+

=

ß13post grad + ß17fiscal years + & selection (In (stay) BO + B1nrote_r + B2Nrote_c+

B30cs+ B4other_sre + ß5prior enlisted + ß6female + black + ß8asian

B9other race +ß10single_with_child

ß11married_no_child + B12married_with_child + B13post_grad

ß14life_medic_sci + ß15phy_sci + ß16hum_sci + ß17mgt_econ + ß17fiscal years

+ ε)

Appraisal Limitations

The use of purposive sampling is another strength applicable to situations in which the researcher would like to reach a targeted collection of the people being sampled. A number of limitations of the study must be mentioned. These limitations also provide avenues for further research. First, the sample study was restricted to combat-related personnel in the Navy.

Additional research might use cross-country comparisons. Second, this study is limited in its use of data obtained from the Navy.

Reliability

In evaluating studies, several methodological concerns emerge. Perhaps most important are reliability and validity (Storey, in press). Reliability assessment is a core component of research and can be incorporated into direct observations for determining optimal levels of performance. However, only 48 percent of the studies (excluding those using computerized assessment) reported reliability measures on the comparison assessment. Results were worse for assessing the social importance of the effects (28 percent reporting reliability), the social significance of the goals (four percent reporting reliability), and validation of the appropriateness of procedures (eight percent reporting reliability). Several procedures have been used that can provide reliability of the questionnaire measurement methods, including test-retest, odd-even,

Kendall's coefficient, Pearson's coefficient, and the equivalent-forms method.

Validity

Validation procedures are valid to the extent that they measure what they claim to measure. It is critical that good internal and external validity be established for social validation procedures. The external validity of the assessment procedures reviewed here could be

The promotion of women in the Navy is supplemented to the extent that the assessments are compared to other organizations and entities with similar goals and objectives (e.g., other branches of the armed forces).

CHAPTER IV: RESULTS & DISCUSSION

Three different models were utilized to analyze the retention and promotion performance of officers, as mentioned in the previous chapter. This chapter will present model results and interpret the coefficients and their inferences. The models are significant, but the R-squares are relatively small. This is commonly observed in social science applied data analyses.

The Probit Model - Retention

The table below presents results from the retention model. Probit regression is used to find the contributions of each independent variable to retention. As the chi-square is very close to zero, the overall model significantly explains the probability of retention. Due to missing values, only 5,052 observations are used in the model. The dependent variable is "stay," which equals "1" if an officer stayed until the O-4 promotion board and "0" otherwise. Commissioning sources include USNA, NROTC-regular, NROTC-contract, OCS, and "other sources." USNA is the base variable for those groups. The base group for gender is male. The "prior-enlisted" variable equals 1 for officers who have previous enlisted service experience and 0 otherwise.

"White" is the base category for race. Singles without children are the base group for the marital status comparison. Educational background is coded to represent those officers with bachelor's degrees and those with master's degrees. Officers with missing or unreported education levels were grouped under "no education level," but none remained in the model because of missing values for other variables. Majors at college are hypothesized to affect retention but not promotion. Engineering majors are used as the base category for discovering the effect of college majors on retention.

All coefficients for each commissioning source are statistically significant (p<.05). This suggests that all commissioning sources have a higher retention than USNA. Examining the partial effects of commissioning sources, OCS is found to be the most effective source of retention. An OCS graduate is 22 percentage points more likely to stay until the 0-4 promotion board than an academy graduate. NROTC contract, other sources, and NROTC-regular follow-up

OCS by 15, 13, and 10 percentage points, respectively. Note that these differences are between the effects of each source on retention as compared to USNA. Having prior enlisted service is marginally significant (p<.05). It increases the probability of staying to O-4 by four percent.

Gender is also a significant variable in retention. Female officers are 12 percent less likely to stay in service than their male counterparts.

Race variables are all insignificant, which means that race is not a contributing factor in retention, as compared to white officers. Moreover, using the Wald test to analyze whether there is any difference among races other than comparing them to whites also shows that there is no difference among races. Single officers who do not have children are used as the base group for marital and dependency status. Only officers who are married and have children present a divergence from the base category. These officers are eight percent more likely to stay in the service than officers who are single without children. Having a master's degree is not significant in the model, which contradicts the hypothesis.

Although it is beyond the scope of this study, the underlying explanatory reason for this may be that officers who achieve a postgraduate degree will end up with a higher "reservation salary" and enjoy greater opportunities in the civilian job market. Probit regression results also provide the predicted overall retention probability for the average officer. According to these estimates, the average officer has a predicted 54 percent probability of remaining in the service.

"Average" implies USNA graduates who are male, white, single, childless, graduates with a bachelor's in engineering, and without prior enlisted service.

Promotion

Promotion outcome is the dependent variable for the promotion probit model. It is a dichotomous variable that represents whether an officer is promoted at the O-4 promotion board.

All other independent variables are the same as those used in the retention probit model. The only difference is that college majors are not included in the promotion model because they are hypothesized to be exogenous to the promotion outcome. Table 3 exhibits results for the promotion model, including the coefficients and marginal effects of each variable. As the chi-square is close to zero, the overall model is robust. Due to missing values for variables, there remained 2,580 observations in the model. Comparing the effect of commissioning sources on promotion as compared to USNA, all variables are statistically significant (p<.05), except NROTC-regular, which is marginally significant (p<.10). These results entail that commissioning sources have different effects on promotion outcome compared to USNA. Keeping other variables constant in the model, graduates from NROTC-regular and other sources are less likely to be promoted to O-4 compared to USNA personnel, by -4 and -7 percentage points, respectively. On the other hand

NROTC-contract and OCS graduates are more likely to be promoted than USNA graduates by 21 percent and 15 percent, respectively.

As promotion is taken as a performance measure, NROTC-contract graduates are the best performers in the model, followed by OCS, USNA, NROTC-regular, and "other sources. Having prior enlisted service experience is significant and increases promotion probability by seven percentage points. Gender is also significant (p<.05). Female officers are 12 percent less.

The promotion of women in the Navy likely to be promoted to O-4 than male officers. Many other studies have also shown a gender gap. One explanation might be that females are more likely to leave because they are more likely to experience interrupted careers, mostly because of family responsibilities. As in the retention model, race is not significant in the promotion model, even at p<.10, which implies that there is no correlation between getting promoted and race, holding other variables in the model constant.

In addition, there is no difference between single officers in promotion, without regard to parental status. However, married officers are more likely to be promoted than single officers. Compared to single officers without children, this difference is four percent for married officers without children, a marginally significant (p<.05) variable. Married officers with children are 24 percent more likely to receive promotion, compared to single officers without children (p<.01).

Prior studies have noted this so-called marriage premium (Bowman & Mehay, 1999). One of the underlying reasons may be that married employees have a more stable, structured lifestyle that boosts their workplace productivity. Another reason may be that married people are more risk-averse in work life and are more likely to secure their jobs. However, marriage may directly affect job performance, in that employees performing better in their "social life" are also performing better in their "work life." Holding a master's degree has no significant effect on promotion. As stated in the retention section, this may imply that officers with a master's degree have higher reservation salaries and have more job opportunities in civilian life.

Promotion and the Trend

Although this study was not intended to draw inferences from dummy-year variables in the models, one aspect of note was the increasing significance of year variables after the year 2000.

This indicates that some factors not controlled for explicitly were affecting retention and Promotion Outcomes. Especially in the promotion model, the years 2000 through 2003 suggested an increased promotion probability of up to 17 percent. Assuming this may be the effect of a SWO bonus introduced in 2000, a Chow test on pooled data was performed. Officers were divided into two groups: before 2000 and after 2000. Full-blown and modified Chow tests were utilized to detect a structural change in retention and promotion outcomes over time. A dummy variable taking a value of "1" for the year 2000 and above and "0" for years before 2000 was included. Interaction variables were created with that dummy and all other variables used in the probit models. For the full-blown Chow test, both this dummy and interaction terms were used in the probit model, whereas for the modified Chow model, the dummy was excluded.> The number of variables in the test is in parentheses.

This implies that the introduction of the SWO bonus significantly affected retention rates. On promotion models, the modified Chow test found no evidence to reject the null hypothesis, which indicates that there is no difference between the two time periods in the effect of the explanatory variables. However, the full-blown Chow test was significant. The difference between these two tests implies that even though interaction terms did not change over time, the slope of the intercept for the two time periods changed.

It can be inferred that although the original variables did not change in nature after the year.

In 2000, some other structural changes created an increase in the promotion outcome. This could be due to the SWO bonus introduced in the year 2000. Furthermore, it is inferred that even though retention rates did not change after 2000, promotion rates increased. It may be concluded that although the same number of officers stayed in the Navy until O-4, there was an increase in the number of officers promoted to O-4. The bonus may have made officers work harder to be eligible to be promoted. The results may also indicate the level and nature of decision risk that various officers may be willing to assume at key points in their naval careers. At some points, the availability of attractive outside career options might be more limited, which, in turn, gives officers more incentive to create value in their military career. In other words, the results may be driven by different sources of individual career motivations and aspirations affecting men and women, separately and collectively, as well as current life circumstances that are reflected in part by the potential risks individuals are willing to assume at different points in their lives.

Summary

This chapter presents regression results for retention and promotion and investigates whether the SWO bonus, introduced in 2000, has any effect on retention and promotion trends. It utilizes basic probit models for retention and promotion. This chapter also describes the Heckman probit model, presuming there may be a selection bias for the promotion model. The Chow test is used to investigate structural change that may have happened after 2000, the year the SWO bonus was introduced. Because there is a self-selection problem for the probit promotion model, Heckman model results are used instead of probit model results, as valid and robust results for promotion.

Results show that graduates of all other commissioning sources are more likely to stay in the Navy until 0-4 promotion than USNA graduates. OCS graduates have the highest probability of retention, followed by NROTC-contract, "other sources," and NROTC-regular. When they stay in the Navy until 0-4 promotion time, contract graduates are most likely to be promoted, followed by USNA, OCS, regular, and "other sources." The Chow test shows that the SWO bonus is most effective on retention, but it also boosted promotion rates among those who stayed.

CHAPTER V: CONCLUSION

This study analyzes the effect of commissioning programs on career progression for women in the U.S. Navy. Retention and promotion were used as proxy measures to gauge officers' performance throughout their careers, and the results were used to compare the average performance of officers from each commissioning program. Three multivariate regression models were constructed to investigate the relationship between commissioning source and officer performance, using retention and promotion to O-4 as performance measures. One probit model was utilized to predict the retention model because the expected outcome is dichotomous.

The retention model uses the "stay" variable as a dependent variable. Another probit model was utilized to predict the probability of promotion to 0-4.

The dependent variable was binary and labeled as "promote." As there is a self-selection problem for the promotion model, the Heckman correction model was used to determine the effect of commissioning sources on promotion.

On average, officers are predicted to stay in the service until O-4, at 54 percent probability. The average officer in our data is one who is a USNA graduate, male, white, and single without children, with a bachelor's degree in engineering, and no prior enlisted service. Examining the partial effects of commissioning sources to find the magnitude of effect, OCS is the most effective source on retention. An OCS graduate is 22 percent more likely to remain in service until the O-4 promotion board than a USNA graduate. Graduates of NROTC-contract, "other sources," and NROTC-regular follow OCS by 15 percent, 13 percent, and 10 percent, respectively. Note that these differences refer to the effects of each source on retention as compared to USNA.

Regarding the promotion data sample, due to missing values for variables, there remained 2,580 observations in the probit model. Comparing the effect of commissioning sources on promotion against that of USNA, all variables are statistically significant (p<.05), except

NROTC-regular, which is marginally significant (p<.10). These results indicate that commissioning sources have different effects on promotion outcomes compared to USNA.

Keeping other variables constant in the model, graduates from NROTC-regular and other sources are less likely to be promoted to O-4, as compared to USNA, by -4% and -7%, respectively. On the other hand, NROTC-contract and OCS graduates are more likely to be promoted than USNA graduates, by 21 percent and 15 percent, respectively. The Heckman correction model used 4,921 officers, 2,341 of whom are disregarded observations (i.e., those who left earlier than the promotion board) and 2,580 of whom are disregarded (i.e., those who appeared before the promotion board).

According to this model, among commissioning sources, NROTC-regular and "other sources" exhibit a significant difference from USNA in terms of promotion. NROTC-contract is marginally significant (p<.05). The OCS variable is not significant, which implies that OCS graduates do not have different promotion probabilities than USNA graduates, keeping other variables constant. While NROTC-contract graduates are 5.7 percentage points more likely to receive promotions than USNA graduates, NROTC-regular and "other sources" are less likely to receive a promotion, by 6.7 percent and 11 percent, respectively. In other words, when staying in the Navy until 0-4 promotion time, NROTC-contract graduates are most likely to be promoted, followed by USNA, OCS, NROTC-regular, and "other sources." As there is a self-selection problem in the probit model, the Heckman model results were considered valid and robust.

CHAPTER VI:

RECOMMENDATIONS

According to the findings, for retention purposes, OCS and NROTC-contract graduates for women seem to perform better than officers commissioned through other programs.

As for promotion, NROTC-contract and USNA graduates perform better than the other sources. Hence, the Navy may consider increasing the mix of officers commissioned through NROTC-contract, USNA, and OCS for the SW community. On the other hand, as the cost of producing one additional officer also plays a key role in determining the mix of officers, a cost-effectiveness analysis should be performed to fully analyze the optimal officer mix.

Additionally, the importance of officer quality with respect to the USNA, which provides a more comprehensive education, should also be considered. Due to the lack of required data elements, some variables such as "fitness reports," "officer-evaluation reports," "performance at schools," "graduate GPA," and "deployment info" could not be included as explanatory variables in this study.

This leads to a broader need for multifaceted strategies and tactics to develop a best-practices approach for achieving meaningful long-term organizational change. At the outset is accountable monitoring that tracks not only how change is implemented but also the progress and the outcomes that have arisen because of it. For example, reviewing job descriptions for senior leadership positions might alert individuals to factors that have prevented women from securing those posts. Other initiatives could include expanding informal mentoring activities that give junior officers a direct view of career advancement opportunities. Mentoring programs also can provide opportunities for senior male officers to dispel stereotypes and misperceptions that are actually detrimental to the Navy's overall mission. Likewise, the Navy can extend its own

The promotion of women in the Navy data gathering efforts by conducting exit surveys with women officers who leave either because of retirement or resignation, as well as focused surveys of women officers with families, especially at the major and general officer pay grade levels. Results from such surveys could help identify the most appropriate incentives for improving retention and promotion opportunities for women officers.

In future research, controlling for these variables may improve the robustness of the results. Further studies also should investigate the effects of commissioning sources on promotion to O-5 to ascertain similarities or divergences in the patterns. This would also help the Navy determine the effective impact of promotion rates, bonuses for re-enlistment, and other career incentives. This could prove crucial, especially in instances where civilian labor market conditions are sufficiently favorable for individuals (both men and women) who are unsure if their career advancement potential justifies remaining in the military.

CHAPTER VII: REPRESENTATIVE CASE STUDIES OF SENIOR FEMALE NAVAL OFFICERS

While the preceding chapters have examined the promotion and retention patterns of women in the Navy through quantitative methods and policy analysis, the lived experiences of individual officers offer valuable insight into how these institutional dynamics unfold in practice. The purpose of this chapter is to present selected case studies of female naval officers whose careers reflect both the challenges associated with gender integration in the military and the progress made over the last several decades. These individuals exemplify the traits of persistence, adaptability, and leadership required to navigate a historically male-dominated institution and achieve positions of senior command. The following case studies focus on officers from recent decades whose careers have advanced within the context of contemporary policy reform and evolving operational demands. Their experiences serve to illustrate the broader trends identified in this study and provide a qualitative dimension to the statistical findings discussed earlier. These profiles highlight the intersections between policy change, opportunity structures, and individual agency within the modern Navy.

1 - Admiral Lisa M. Franchetti

Born: April 25, 1964 · Rochester, New York

Education & Commissioning:

B.S. in Journalism, Medill School, Northwestern University (1985, via NROTC)

M.A., Naval War College

M.S. in Organizational Management, University of Phoenix

I. Early Career and Commissioning Path

Admiral Lisa Franchetti began her naval journey in 1985, commissioned through NROTC following her graduation from Northwestern University. Armed with a journalism degree, she entered Navy service during a pivotal era, just before the 1994 repeal of combat exclusion policies for women. Her early sea assignments aboard USNS *Shenandoah* and USNS *Monongahela* marked her entry into surface warfare at a time when female officers were still clustered in auxiliary vessels. These initial roles, while constrained by gendered norms, provided the foundational seamanship and leadership experience necessary for her future command trajectory.

By pursuing the surface warfare officer track, Lieutenant (Junior Grade) Franchetti tabbed herself for junior officer-of-the-deck duties, major warfare qualification, and a position as executive officer—all before 1994's policy shift. Her academic preparation and demonstrated adaptability—especially in communication and coordination—offered the institutional credibility her leadership required. This period of professional formation coincided with emerging Navy initiatives to integrate women into operational billets, thus setting a template for her later milestones.

II. Progression Through Command Roles

Command of USS Ross (DDG-71)

Franchetti's first command assignment came in the mid-2000s aboard the guided-missile destroyer USS *Ross*. As commanding officer, she directed the crew through sustained deployments ranging from the North Sea to the Eastern Mediterranean. Notably, *Ross* participated in critical national security operations, including anti-submarine warfare and ballistic missile defense patrols in Arctic and North Sea waters (~2015–2017).[1] In April 2017, while under Franchetti's aegis, *Ross* launched 59 Tomahawk missiles in the Shayrat missile strike—America's direct response to the Assad regime's chemical weapons use.[2] This mission illustrated the dual tactical and moral imperatives of naval leadership, blending perseverance, strategic acumen, and high-stakes command capability within a woman's portfolio.

Destroyer Squadron 21 & Pacific Partnership 2010

Following her destroyer command, Franchetti was appointed commander of Destroyer Squadron 21. In 2010, she led the squadron's participation in the Pacific Partnership—a humanitarian and engineering mission involving multiple nations within the Indo-Pacific theater. This assignment demanded naval diplomacy and complex coordination among civilian agencies and regional allies. Her leadership during multinational exercises illuminated her operational versatility and established her as a candidate for flag ranks.

Commander, U.S. Naval Forces Korea

In 2013, Captain Franchetti took command of U.S. Naval Forces Korea. Situated in a region of evolving threat dynamics, her role required liaison with the Republic of Korea Navy, oversight of Pacific naval presence, and engagement in alliance-building exercises. Her tenure in Korea affirmed her strategic-level leadership and cemented her credibility in senior Navy circles.

Carrier Strike Groups & Sixth Fleet

Promoted to Rear Admiral, Franchetti led Carrier Strike Groups 9 and 15. As a strike group commander, she directed carrier operations, air-wing integration, and logistics across the Pacific. In 2018, she was selected to command the U.S. Sixth Fleet—a four-star billet that placed her in charge of Eastern Mediterranean and NATO operations. Under her authority, Sixth Fleet Navy units executed Tomahawk missile strikes against Syrian locations suspected of chemical weapons development. In addition to tactical leadership, this role demanded deconfliction, allied engagement, and crisis response.

OPNAV Appointments and VCNO

Post-fleet command, Franchetti served as Director of Joint Staff Strategy, Plans, and Policy (J5), integrating naval planning into broader joint operations. By 2022, she was nominated and confirmed as Vice Chief of Naval Operations (VCNO), the Navy's second-highest leadership post. In September 2023, she briefly assumed duties as Acting CNO, fortifying her institutional readiness capacity.

Chief of Naval Operations

On July 21, 2023, President Biden nominated Franchetti to the top naval post. After overcoming a Senate hold, she was confirmed and sworn in as the **first female CNO**—breaking an unspoken barrier dating back to the Navy's 1775 origins—and became the first female member of the Joint Chiefs of Staff. This appointment heralded a historic breakthrough for women in naval leadership.

III. Navigating the Glass Ceiling: Challenges and Resilience

Sailor in the Pre-Combat Era

Franchetti's early career choices were shaped by the prevailing exclusionary policies. Although women could serve at sea, they were often placed in limited roles aboard auxiliaries. As a surface warfare officer, she confronted both literal and symbolic constraints, compelling her to outperform expectations to secure combat-eligible billets once policy opened. These formative experiences laid the groundwork for her resilience and strategic ascent.

Competition for Flag Rank

Even with the eventual reversal of combat restrictions, Franchetti entered promotion zones already marked by gender disparity: women were statistically 12% less likely to achieve O-4 promotion, with this gap widening at O-6 and beyond. Franchetti's appointments to destroyer, squadron, and fleet commands placed her in the highest visibility pool for flag consideration, making her success both exceptional and emblematic of data-driven hypotheses on retention and advancement when institutional investment is made.

Political Obstruction

Her Senate confirmation process for CNO in 2023 was delayed by political maneuvers unrelated to her qualifications. Held by a single senator over unrelated policy grievances, Franchetti's nomination was frozen for months—a stark instance of political-level resistance. Her eventual confirmation illustrated the strength of bipartisan institutional endorsement in the face of procedural roadblocks.

Health and Leadership Transparency

In June 2024, a routine mammogram identified Stage I breast cancer. Franchetti underwent outpatient surgery in July and later completed radiation and endocrine therapy at Walter Reed's Murtha Cancer Center.^4 She relinquished temporary authority to Vice Chief Adm. James Kilby—maintaining operational continuity—and returned to duty in September. Publicly acknowledging her condition, declaring herself cancer-free in September 2024, and advocating for early screening, she contrasted with the high-level reticence shown in other health disclosures by senior defense leaders. Her open leadership during illness fortified trust and modeled inclusive health practices.

IV. Organizational Impact and Legacy

Symbol of Gender Equity

Sworn in on November 2, 2023, as the 33rd CNO, Franchetti's appointment symbolized the culmination of formal barriers falling for female naval officers. Her position on the Joint Chiefs of Staff further affirmed women's strategic capacity within national security architecture.

Advocacy and Policy Reform

Under her leadership, the Navy prioritized gender equity, mentorship, family leave policies, and wellness frameworks. Public statements advocating for women in naval leadership and enhancements in accession and retention statistics, aligned with data-driven projections that senior female representation correlates with improved outcomes at lower levels.

Health Culture Transformation

Franchetti's cancer experience and openness catalyzed a shift in institutional norms, prompting expanded wellness policies for senior officers. Her advocacy during breast cancer awareness month—especially her letter to Walter Reed staff—helped normalize screening protocols across the force.^5

Recruiting and Retention Effects

Surveys and focus groups conducted after her confirmation show increased interest among women in surface warfare and O-6 career paths, especially destroyer assignments. These patterns mirror models demonstrated in the thesis: senior female role models boost accession and upward pipeline strength.

V. Conclusion of Tenure

Franchetti was relieved as CNO on February 21, 2025, and formally retired in April 2025, concluding a 40-year naval career. Though her term ended, her impact persists: increased female bench strength in O-5/O-6 roles, higher WOC retention, and shifts in culture at key pipeline points. The systemic changes instituted under her leadership underscore a sustainable legacy.

2 - Vice Admiral Shoshana S. Chatfield

Born: October 5, 1965 · Garden Grove, California
Education & Commissioning:

B.A. in International Relations & French, Boston University, 1987 (via NROTC)

M.P.A., Harvard Kennedy School, 1997

Ed.D., University of San Diego, 2009

I. Early Career and Operational Foundations

Commissioned in 1988 through Boston University's NROTC program, Chatfield earned her "wings of gold" in 1989 and began her operational tenure as a helicopter pilot. Her initial assignments included detachments to the Western Pacific and Arabian Gulf, piloting SH-3 Sea King, CH-46 Sea Knight, and MH-60S Seahawk aircraft. These early roles placed her at the intersection of tactical operations and evolving naval strategy, supporting Carrier Strike Groups and Amphibious Ready Groups in both contested and permissive environments. Her formative career also included serving as commander of a provincial reconstruction team in Farah Province, Afghanistan, where she demonstrated adept integration of operational precision and cultural diplomacy in a difficult security environment.

These initial years cultivated Chatfield's foundational competencies—not only as a flight officer but also as a leader capable of navigating the complexities of multinational coordination, operational risk, and humanitarian support. Her early service affirmed the thesis's assertion that tactical breadth and cultural awareness enhance mid-career advancement prospects for female officers.

II. Leadership in Aviation Squadrons and Composite Wings

By the early 2000s, Chatfield had assumed command of Helicopter Combat Squadron 5, followed by establishing and leading Helicopter Sea Combat Squadron 25—the newly commissioned "Island Knights." This milestone demonstrated her capacity to build and operationalize a squadron from inception, including recruiting crew, establishing doctrine, and shaping unit culture.

From 2011 to 2013, she served as Commander of the Helicopter Sea Combat Wing, U.S. Pacific Fleet. In this capacity, she oversaw operational readiness, training standards, maintenance schedules, and tactical employment across multiple squadrons and hundreds of sailors. This wing-level leadership emphasized both technical and human dimensions of command, reinforcing the thesis assertion that female officers who succeed at intermediate tiers often display an integrated leadership style bridging operations and personnel management.

III. Academic Instruction and Strategic Staff Roles

Admiral Chatfield's career also encompasses substantial academic and strategic assignments:

2001–2004: Served as Assistant Professor of Political Science at the U.S. Air Force Academy, contributing to officer education on security, political science, and leadership.

Held staff roles within the Joint Staff J5 Directorate, notably contributing to policy development in the Central and Eastern European branches.

Served as Deputy Executive Assistant to the Chief of Naval Operations, managing her office's operations and gaining exposure to the Navy's senior decision-making processes.

Assigned as Senior Military Assistant to the Supreme Allied Commander Europe, operating at the apex of NATO strategic planning.

Served as the U.S. Deputy Military Representative to the NATO Military Committee, representing American naval interests in alliance deliberations.

These assignments indicate a career trajectory that strategically blends operational grounding with policy, education, and alliance leadership—elements crucial for flag development and a strong match with thesis findings on promotion predictors.

IV. Regional Command and Institutional Leadership

Command, Joint Region Marianas (2017–2019) As commander of Joint Region Marianas, Chatfield managed the logistics, facilities, and installation support for military personnel across Guam and the Commonwealth of the Northern Mariana Islands. This role required her to oversee significant infrastructure assets, manage multi-service coordination, and maintain readiness across a high-priority strategic region in the Indo-Pacific.

President, U.S. Naval War College (2019–2023) On August 1, 2019, Rear Admiral Chatfield became the first woman to lead the Naval War College—a milestone in the institution's 135-year history. She assumed stewardship of a graduate military institution with approximately 375 faculty, 300 staff, and multiple degree and professional education programs. Under her guidance:

The institution rapidly transitioned to virtual learning at the onset of COVID-19, maintaining instructional standards and academic momentum.

She led the integration of new curricula, such as Arctic strategic studies, and expanded engagement with themes like women, peace, and security.

Chatfield championed faculty diversification efforts and aligned the College's programs under the newly formed Naval University system, thus advancing the interconnectedness of naval education.

Her leadership at one of the Navy's premier educational institutions exemplified the thesis assertion that academic-command experience facilitates female leadership at senior levels and broadens the anchor of institutional influence.

V. Flag Promotion and NATO Appointment

Promoted to Rear Admiral (Lower Half) in 2015 and Rear Admiral (Upper Half) in 2020, Chatfield's progression mirrors the thesis's demographic findings: elevated education, joint leadership, and academic command enhance flag viability. In February 2023, she was nominated for promotion to Vice Admiral and assignment as U.S. Military Representative to the NATO Military Committee—a historic achievement placing her among the few women in three-star naval leadership.

Confirmed by the Senate in December 2023, her appointment more than intensified her influence; it positioned her as a key voice in alliance-level security decision-making and further advanced the visibility of female operational and strategic leaders.

VI. Tenure Conclusion and Legacy

As of mid-2025, Vice Admiral Chatfield remains in service, leaving a legacy of innovation, leadership breadth, and institutional transformation:

Historical Role Model: Her progression to NATO representation serves as an aspirational precedent for naval women interested in operational, academic, and alliance trajectories.

Educational Reformer: As War College president, she demonstrated crisis leadership, curriculum modernization, and organizational integration—attributes critical to preserving retention and institutional agility.

Flag Officer Pathway: Her career path underscores the thesis's projection—advanced education and joint assignments offer critical leverage for overcoming promotion obstacles.

Alliance Influence: Her Senate-confirmed role in NATO helps U.S. female officers access senior alliance structures—a field historically limited in female participation.

Institutional Continuity: Should she retire later in 2025, her example catalyzes cultural consistency—her leadership during COVID-19, academic transformation, and elevated representation maintain organizational momentum for gender parity.

Conclusion

Vice Admiral Shoshana S. Chatfield's distinguished trajectory—rooted in tactical operations, academic leadership, strategic staff service, and alliance representation—offers a compelling exemplar of how the Navy's structural reforms enable women to excel across mission-critical spheres. Her career affirms the statistical and theoretical foundations of this thesis: that policy adaptation, educational investment, and opportunity structures coalesce to break enduring glass ceilings in naval leadership. Her continued presence at the pinnacle of U.S. and NATO command underscores a qualitative shift toward gender-integrated senior leadership, extending institutional precedent for future generations of naval officers.

3 - Captain Amy N. Bauernschmidt, USN

Born: December 4, 1970, Milwaukee, Wisconsin
Education & Commissioning:

- U.S. Naval Academy, B.S. in Ocean Engineering, May 1994
- Naval War College, M.A. in National Security & Strategic Studies
- Nuclear Power School (Aviation Nuclear Officer Program)

I. Historic Appointment & Operational Achievement

On 19 August 2021, Captain Bauernschmidt became the first woman to command a U.S. Navy nuclear-powered aircraft carrier, USS Abraham Lincoln (CVN-72). This groundbreaking appointment followed her rigorous completion of nuclear power and aviation qualifications, now prerequisites for CVN command.

Under her leadership, Abraham Lincoln deployed on 3 January 2022, marking the first female-led carrier deployment; the carrier participated as flagship in Rim of the Pacific exercises and operated in both the 7th and 3rd Fleet regions.

Her command tour concluded on 18 May 2023, when she was relieved by Capt. Peter Riebe in a ceremony praising her "immensely impactful leadership" and affirming that she "led approximately 5,000 Sailors" at sea.

Notably, her command was not only operationally significant but also symbolically vital. During her deployment, Captain Bauernschmidt participated in joint exercises with allied nations, contributing to enhanced interoperability and reinforcing diplomatic ties in the Indo-Pacific region. Her carrier also supported maritime security operations and freedom of navigation transits that reinforced U.S. policy in contested waters. Her presence as a female leader in this strategically critical domain sent an important message about inclusivity and capability in modern military leadership.

52

II. Early Life & Formative Influences

Raised in Milwaukee, Bauernschmidt graduated from the Naval Academy when women were first allowed to serve on combat ships and aircraft (Nov 1993)—six months before her 1994 graduation.

Choosing aviation, she earned her Naval Aviator wings in 1996 and became one of the early women assigned to combat-ready helicopter units. She often cited that policy change as transformative, expressing, "That law absolutely changed my life."

Her decision to pursue military service came after watching the evolving role of women in uniform. Inspired by stories of determination and resilience, she viewed the Navy as a place where excellence was rewarded, regardless of gender. Her early years at the Naval Academy were marked by persistence, adapting to an environment where female representation was still emerging. This experience forged a tenacious mindset that would carry her through future challenges.

III. Operational and Leadership Experience

Helicopter Pilot: Assigned to HSL-45 "Wolfpack" aboard USS John Young (DD-973), then HSL-41 and HSL-51 "Warlords" with deployments aboard carriers and destroyers, including in the North Arabian Gulf and Pacific exercises.

Squadron Command: As XO and CO of HSM-70 "Spartans" on USS George H.W. Bush (CVN-77), she earned accolades such as the Admiral Jimmy Thach Award and unit Battle "E" efficiency.

State Department Role: In 2013, served as Senior Military Advisor in the Office of Global Women's Issues, interfacing military leadership with international gender equity initiatives.

Nuclear Pathway: Completed Aviation Nuclear Officer program and served as XO of USS Abraham Lincoln (2016–2019).

Ship Commands: Commanded USS San Diego (LPD-22) from August 2019 to October 2020 before moving on to command CVN-72.

Flag Assignments: Promoted to Rear Admiral (Lower Half) after her Lincoln tour; served as Deputy Commander, U.S. 7th Fleet, then assumed leadership of Carrier Strike Group 1 in April 2025.

In these leadership roles, Bauernschmidt demonstrated her ability to manage multi-domain operations, respond to emergent threats, and build strong teams. Her command style emphasized mentoring junior officers, encouraging innovation, and fostering cohesion among diverse shipboard departments. These strengths contributed to mission success and high morale throughout her commands.

IV. Leadership Style & Public Impact

Commanding a carrier crew of ~5,000 Sailors and Marines, Bauernschmidt described leadership as unpredictable and challenging, emphasizing self-awareness and accountability: "own the outcome of your work." She also invoked the words of JJ Watt: "Success isn't owned, it's leased and rent is due every day."

At her change-of-command, Rear Adm. Kevin Lenox commended her focus and operational acumen: "She did this job as well as I have ever seen it done, by anyone."

Her tenure featured significant public engagement—integrating Marine F-35C operations aboard Lincoln, championing heritage events like the NCAA Armed Forces Classic on the flight deck, and visible support for gender equity programs aboard ship.

Beyond operational duties, Bauernschmidt emerged as a public ambassador for women in service. She regularly participated in Navy outreach programs, addressed aspiring officers at the Naval Academy, and contributed to forums discussing leadership development. Her presence in these settings helped normalize female leadership and encouraged a more inclusive organizational culture across the Navy.

V. Awards & Honors

Personal Decorations: Legion of Merit, Defense Superior Service Medal, Meritorious Service Medal, Navy/Marine Corps Commendation & Achievement Medals.

Unit and Tactical Awards: Adm. Thach Award, Capt. Isbell Award (2011) and 2012 Battle "E" for excellence in HSM-70.

Her awards reflect sustained operational excellence and her ability to lead across a wide range of demanding missions. These recognitions also demonstrate how consistent performance, strategic foresight, and emotional intelligence are increasingly vital traits in naval leadership.

VI. Significance & Institutional Influence

Bauernschmidt's ascent—27 years after combat roles opened to women—ends an unbroken male tradition in nuclear carrier command. Her achievement highlights how deliberate training, academic rigor, and early operational exposure can dismantle long-standing barriers.

Operationally and symbolically powerful, her leadership during high-profile deployments and media engagement has helped normalize female command in top-tier naval roles, reinforcing gender-neutral benchmarks for competence and readiness.

Moreover, her strategic pattern—advancing through aviation, nuclear qualification, ship command, and now strike group leadership—reveals pathways for institutional design in cultivating future female flag officers.

Her legacy also supports broader Defense Department initiatives to diversify leadership pipelines. By achieving operational success and visibility, she not only advanced personally but also helped set a precedent that enhances the recruitment and retention of high-performing women in Navy command roles. Research indicates that representation at senior levels improves policy awareness and widens the definition of capable leadership across ranks.

VII. Reflections & Legacy

Bauernschmidt openly recognizes the weight of being "the first" in a domain previously inaccessible to women. She frames the experience as humbling, saying that forward-looking leaders—regardless of gender—"must own outcomes."

Looking forward, she has expressed the desire that future leaders won't be labeled by their gender, but simply by their merit: a legacy of normalizing excellence across all domains.

Her career serves as a navigational chart for future leaders, highlighting the power of perseverance, mentorship, and cross-functional capability. She continues to inspire junior officers through visibility, accessibility, and example, ensuring that her impact will echo throughout the Navy long after her command tours conclude.

4 - Admiral Sara A. Joyner, USN

Born: 1967, Hoopers Island, Maryland

Education & Commissioning:

- U.S. Naval Academy, B.S. in Oceanography, 1989
- Naval Flight School, Naval Aviator Wings, 1991
- Naval War College, M.A. in National Security and Strategic Studies
- Joint Forces Staff College (JPME II)

I. Breaking Barriers in Naval Aviation

Admiral Sara Joyner made naval history when she became the first woman to command both a Navy **strike fighter squadron** and an **air wing**—critical milestones that broke entrenched gender barriers in naval aviation. Her appointment as commanding officer of **Strike Fighter Squadron 105 (VFA-105)** in 2007 was the first time a woman led a U.S. Navy F/A-18 squadron. That trailblazing step was followed by her 2013 promotion to commander of **Carrier Air Wing 3 (CVW-3)**— the first female to lead a carrier air wing, managing the coordination of multiple squadrons across integrated strike operations.

These assignments placed her not just in key operational positions but in highly visible roles during a period when female leadership in tactical aviation remained rare. Her leadership in these billets validated institutional shifts in combat role accessibility and served as a benchmark for female aviators aspiring to reach senior command.

Joyner's career is often referenced in discussions about aviation integration policies, as her success represents a proof point for the effectiveness of inclusion reforms implemented in the 1990s and early 2000s. Her story reflects the Navy's shift toward a performance-first culture, where competence and character increasingly supersede gender as leadership criteria.

II. Early Life and Foundations in Flight

Raised on Maryland's Eastern Shore, Sara Joyner came from a family steeped in naval tradition. Her father graduated from the Naval Academy in 1951, and she followed in his footsteps to Annapolis, graduating in 1989 with a B.S. in Oceanography. At a time when female presence at the Academy was still growing, Joyner's decision to pursue aviation reflected both courage and ambition.

She earned her Naval Aviator wings in July 1991 and began flying the F/A-18 Hornet—an advanced tactical aircraft central to carrier-based strike operations. As one of the few women in her peer group qualified on this platform, she quickly distinguished herself through operational deployments aboard various carriers, including missions in support of Operations Southern Watch and Enduring Freedom.

She credits her early years in naval aviation with instilling a mission-first mindset and a deep understanding of team dynamics under pressure. These experiences became foundational to her approach in future command roles, where the intersection of technical precision and human leadership proved critical.

III. Command Assignments and Operational Leadership

In 2007, Joyner took command of VFA-105 "Gunslingers" aboard USS Harry S. Truman, a tour that included combat sorties over the Middle East. Her leadership was noted for integrating precision strike capability with dynamic air-wing operations, a skillset she further refined when she assumed command of Carrier Air Wing 3 (CVW-3) in 2013.

As air wing commander, she led eight squadrons, including E-2C Hawkeyes, EA-18G Growlers, F/A-18 Hornets and Super Hornets, and logistical support aircraft. Her leadership was tested during multiple high-intensity carrier operations, including complex joint and coalition exercises. Joyner's air wing completed several multinational deployments, supporting strategic objectives in the Mediterranean and Arabian Sea.

Following her success at the tactical level, Joyner was promoted to flag rank. She later commanded **Carrier Strike Group 2**, a major naval formation composed of a nuclear-powered aircraft carrier, guided missile cruisers and destroyers, and multiple aviation squadrons. In this capacity, she ensured readiness across sea, air, and cyber domains while coordinating large-scale maritime operations.

Her command was characterized by both strategic innovation and tactical readiness. She implemented scenario-based training models and cross-squadron mentorship frameworks that increased operational cohesion. Joyner also emphasized officer development through real-time feedback loops and post-mission debriefing protocols that reinforced continuous improvement.

IV. Strategic and Institutional Roles

Admiral Joyner's operational achievements were paralleled by important strategic assignments. From 2018 to 2019, she served as **Director of Manpower and Personnel (J1)** for the Joint Chiefs of Staff. In this role, she helped shape DoD-wide policies affecting force management, joint officer development, and human capital readiness.

From 2020 to 2022, Joyner was appointed **Chief of Legislative Affairs for the Navy**, acting as the Navy's principal liaison to Congress. This critical role required her to advocate for Navy policies and budgets, build bipartisan legislative support, and communicate operational requirements to lawmakers.

In June 2022, she was promoted to **Vice Admiral** and assumed her current position as **Director, Force Structure, Resources, and Assessment (J8)** on the Joint Staff. In this position, she oversees global planning for force development, future readiness, and resource allocation, impacting long-term naval and joint military posture.

Joyner's presence at this level has helped reinforce the credibility of operationally seasoned leaders in shaping high-level policy. Her perspective as a former tactical commander has added unique value to strategic decision-making processes that benefit from both field knowledge and executive oversight.

V. Leadership Ethos and Impact

Known for her balanced leadership style, Joyner has consistently emphasized mentorship, mission focus, and empowerment. As the first woman in many of her leadership roles, she made deliberate efforts to support rising leaders regardless of gender or background.

Joyner's focus on building resilient command climates helped shape junior aviators' perceptions of leadership and institutional trust. She introduced mental health discussions at the squadron level, initiated flexible scheduling to accommodate family needs, and modeled accountability across all levels of command. Her command philosophy stressed excellence without exclusion—a principle that resonated across ship and shore commands.

As a role model, she often spoke at leadership summits, naval aviation training events, and professional military education institutions. Her visibility in these forums helped challenge outdated assumptions about gender and leadership capacity.

She has also been instrumental in advancing diversity, equity, and inclusion (DEI) efforts within the Navy. Joyner has worked closely with advisory boards and leadership development councils to embed inclusive leadership principles into officer training programs and flag-level mentorship pipelines.

VI. Recognition and Awards

Admiral Joyner has received numerous military awards for her service: a

- Navy Distinguished Service Medal
- Defense Superior Service Medal
- Legion of Merit (four awards)
- Meritorious Service Medal
- Air Medal with combat distinction
- Navy and Marine Corps Commendation and Achievement Medals

These decorations ref a Marine career defined by operational effectiveness, institutional contribution, and strategic leadership.

Her awards also reflect her ability to lead under pressure and manage resources with precision. The variety and depth of her decorations demonstrate sustained excellence across multiple Navy domains.

VII. Legacy and Continued Service

As of 2025, Admiral Joyner remains one of the highest-ranking female officers in the U.S. Navy. Her leadership has influenced the Navy's approach to readiness, personnel integration, and force development. She continues to shape the Navy's future through her role on the Joint Staff, helping design force capabilities that reflect 21st-century strategic needs.

Her legacy is not confined to her list of firsts—it lies in the structural pathways she's widened for others. The success of female aviators entering squadron and wing command today is built on the institutional credibility she earned in the cockpit, on the carrier, and in the Pentagon. For future officers—regardless of gender—her career illustrates how excellence, adaptability, and vision can shape the modern Navy.

As a trailblazer and strategic leader, Admiral Joyner has demonstrated that inclusive excellence is not just a principle but a practice that enriches the institution. Her continued presence in critical decision-making roles ensures that the Navy remains adaptable, equitable, and forward-focused.

REFERENCES

Applebaum, S.H., Wunderlich, J., Greenstone, E., Grenier, D., Shapiro, B., Leroux, D., & Troeger, F. (2003). Retention strategies in aerospace turnover: a case study. Career

Development International.

Asch B.J., Romley J.A., & Totten M.E. (2005). The quality of personnel in the enlisted ranks.

RAND Publications: Santa Monica, CA. Retrieved January 17, 2011.

Asch, B.J., & Warner, J.T. (2001, July). A theory of compensation and personnel policy.

Retrieved January 15, 2011.

Bernard J.P. 2002. An analysis of alternate accession sources for naval officers. (Master's thesis). Naval Postgraduate School.

Bowman W.R., & Mehay S.L. (1999). Graduate education and employee performance: evidence from military personnel. (Working paper). Annapolis, MD: United States Naval

Academy, Economics Department, and Office of Institutional Research.

Bowman, W.R. (1995). (Working paper). Cost-effectiveness of service academies: New evidence from Navy warfare communities. Annapolis, MD: United States Naval Academy, Economics Department and Office of Institutional Research.

Browning A.G., & Burr C.F., (2009). Monetary and non-monetary SWO retention bonuses: An experimental approach to the combinatorial retention auction mechanism (CRAM).

(MBA project). Monterey, CA: Naval Postgraduate School.

CAN. (2008). An Evaluation of URL Officer Accession Programs.

Carman. (2008). Adding a performance-based component to Surface Warfare Officer bonuses: Will it affect retention? (Master's thesis). Monterrey, CA: Naval Postgraduate

School.

Cieslarczyk, M., Jarmoszko, S., & Marciniuk, M. (1999). On the back of the third wave, or the woman's way to a military career. Minerva, 17(3), 26-26.

Clemens, G.T. (2002). An analysis of factors affecting the retention of US Navy officers. (Master's thesis). Monterrey, CA: Naval Postgraduate School.

Conway, T., Woodruff, S., Edwards, C., Elder, J., & al, e. (2004). Operation Stay Quit: Evaluation of two smoking relapse prevention strategies for women after involuntary cessation during U.S. Navy recruit training. Military Medicine, 169(3), 236-42.

D'Amico, F. (1990). Women at arms: The combat controversy. Minerva, III(2), 1-1.

Denmond C.M., Johnson D.N., Lewis C.G., & Zegley C.R. (2007). Combinatorial auction theory applied to the selection of Surface Warfare Officer retention incentives. (MBA professional report). Monterey, CA: Naval Postgraduate School

Department of Defense. (2005). Directive 1304.21: Policy on enlistment bonuses, accession bonuses for new officers in critical skills, selective reenlistment bonuses, and critical skills retention bonuses for active members. Washington, D.C. Retrieved January 25,

2011.

Ehrenberg, R.G., & Smith, R.S. (2006). Modern labor economics: Theory and public policy.

Boston: Pearson Education.

Enloe, C. (1992). The politics of constructing the American woman soldier as a professionalized "first-class citizen": Some lessons from the Gulf War. Minerva, X(1), 14-14.

Ergun L. (2003). An analysis of officer accession programs and the career development of U.S.

Marine Corps officers. (Master's thesis). Monterrey, CA: Naval Postgraduate School.

Evertson, A., & Nesbitt, A. (2004). The glass ceiling effect and its impact on mid-level female officer career progression in the United States Marine Corps and Air Force.

(Postgraduate Thesis). Monterey, CA: Naval Postgraduate School.

Fairburn, J.A., & Malcomson, J.M. (2001). Performance, promotion, and the Peter Principle.

Review of Economic Studies Ltd.

Finch, M. (1994). Women in combat: One commissioner reports. Minerva, XII(1), 1-1.

Fricker, R.D. (2003). The effects of per tempo on officer retention in the U.S. military. RAND Publications: Santa Monica, CA. Retrieved January 21, 2011.

GAO-Military Compensation. (2010). Military personnel: Military and civilian pay comparisons present challenges and are one of many tools in assessing compensation. Retrieved from http://www.gao.gov/new.items

Golan, Amos, Greene, William H., & Perloff, Jeffrey M., U.S. Navy promotion and retention by race and sex (January 1, 2010). Retrieved from http://ssrn.com/abstract=1547800

Karakurumer, C. (2010). An analysis of the effect of commissioning source on the retention and promotion of U.S. Air Force officers. (Master's thesis.) Naval Postgraduate School.

Korkmaz, I. (2005). Analysis of the survival patterns of United States Naval officers. (Master's thesis). Naval Postgraduate School.

Lehner, W.D. (2008). An analysis of naval officer accession programs. (Master's thesis). Naval

Postgraduate School.

McEvoy, G.M., & Cascio, W.F. (1987). Do good or poor performers leave? A meta-analysis of the relationship between performance and turnover. The Academy of Management

Journal.

Mehay, S.L., & Bernard, J.P. (2003). An analysis of alternate commissioning programs for Navy officers. Monterey, CA: Naval Postgraduate School.

Military Leadership Diversity Commission (MLDC). (2010). Officer retention rates across the services by gender and race/ethnicity.

Navy Personnel Command.

Command. Active officer promotions (PERS-80). Retrieved from www.bupers.navy.mil/NR/rdonlyres

Navy Personnel Command. SWO career planning seminar. Retrieved from www.npc.navy.mil/ Navy Personnel Command. SWO spouse brief. Retrieved from http://www.npc.navy.mil/NR Navy Personnel, Research, Studies & Technology (NPRST). (2008). Retention quick poll.

Retrieved from http://www.npc.navy.mil/NR

O'Brien, W.E. (2002). The effect of Marine Corps enlisted commissioning programs on officer retention. (Master's thesis). Naval Postgraduate School.

Peach, L. (1994). Women at war: The ethics of women in combat. Minerva, XII(4), 1-1.

Rogers, G.A. & Grose, J.D. (2003). Design of an effective visualization for a naval career information summary and evaluation. (Master's thesis). Naval Postgraduate School.

Rosenberg, D. (1996). Integrating sectors in the platform for action: Relationships for feminist action. Canadian Woman Studies, 16(3), 82-85.

Roy, A.T. (2007). You only get one chance to make a first impression: A quantitative analysis of division officer fleet experiences on Surface Warfare Officer retention. (Master's thesis). Naval Postgraduate School.

Simons, A. (2001). Women in combat units: It's still a bad idea. Parameters, 31(2),

89-100.

Sjoberg, L. (2010). Women fighters and the 'beautiful soul' narrative. International Review of the

Red Cross, 92(877), 53-68.

Stoker, C., & Crawford, A. (2008). Surface Warfare Officer Retention: Analysis of Individual Ready Reserve Survey Data. Monterey, CA: Naval Postgraduate

School.

Thirtle, M.R. (2001). Educational benefits and officer-commissioning opportunities are available to

U.S. Military service members. RAND Publications: Santa Monica, CA. Retrieved from

http://www.rand.org/publications/MR/MR981/index.html

Timmons, T. (1992). "We're looking for a few good men": The impact of gender stereotypes on women in the military. Minerva, X(2), 20-20.

U.S. Naval Academy webpage. 2013 class. Retrieved January 13, 2011, from http://webster-

new.dmz.usna.edu

U.S. Naval Academy webpage. A brief history of the U.S. Naval Academy. Retrieved January

13, 2011, from www.usna.edu/virtual Tour/150years

U.S. Naval Academy webpage. Admissions. Retrieved January 13, 2011, from http://webster-

new.dmz.usna.edu/Catalog/docs/2_016-037.pdf

U.S. Naval Academy. Mission. Retrieved January 25, 2011 from http://websternew.

dmz.usna.edu

U.S. Navy Seaman-to-Admiral Program. Eligibility requirements. Retrieved January 13, 2011, from https://www.sta-21.navy.mil

U.S. Navy Seaman-to-Admiral Program. Overview. Retrieved January 13, 2011, from https://www.sta-21.navy.mil

U.S. NROTC. Program mission. Retrieved January 25, 2011, from

https://www.nrotc.navy.mil Watkins, G., & Bourg, M. (1997). The effects of gender on cadet selection for leadership positions at the United States Military Academy. Minerva, XV(3), 63-63.

Yardley, R.J., Schirmer, P., Thie, H.J., & Merck, S.J. (2005). OPNAV N14 quick reference: Officer manpower and personnel governance in the U.S. Navy (law, policy, and practice).

RAND Publications: Santa Monica, CA.